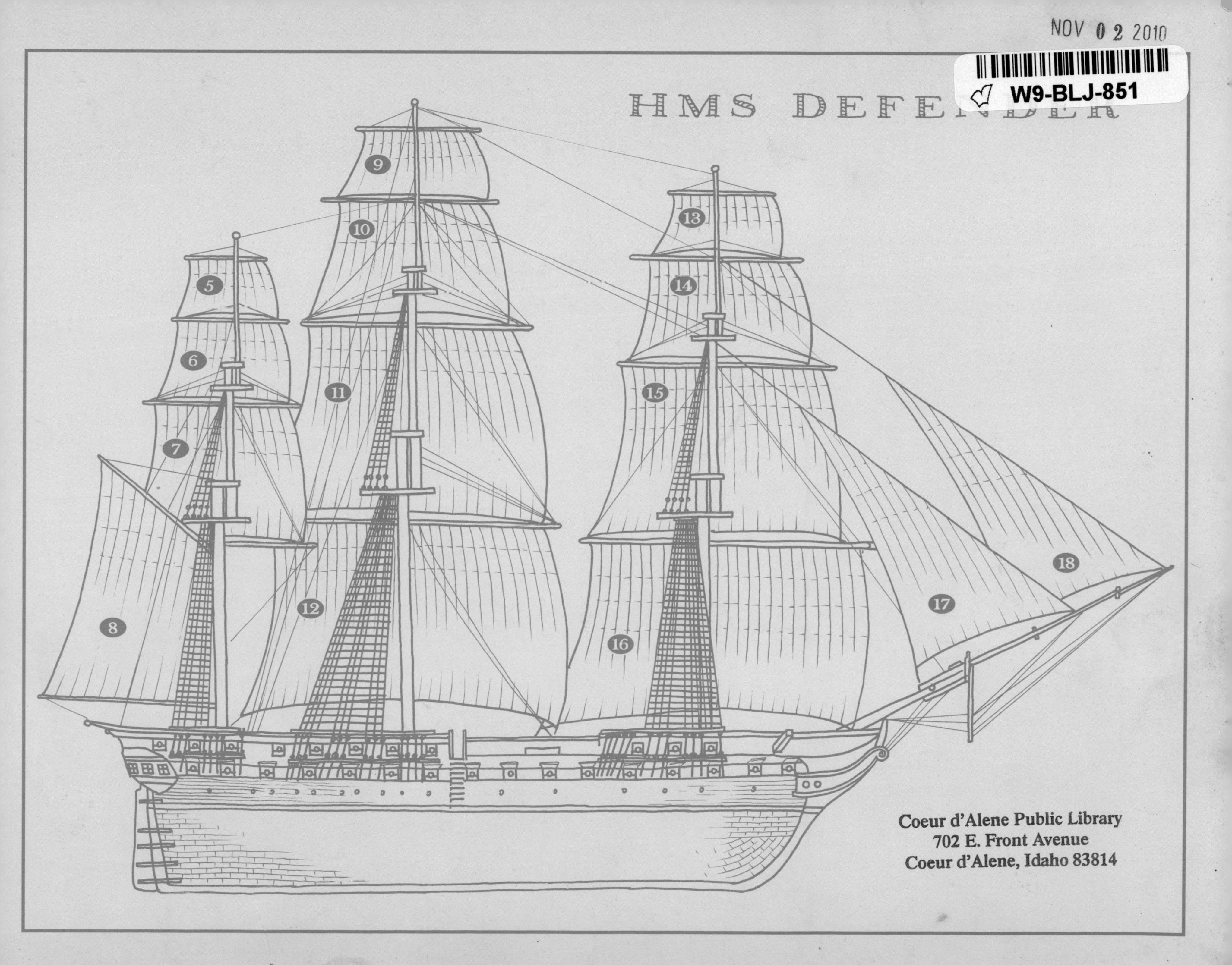
HMS DEFENDER
9
10
5
6
11
7
8
12
13
14
15
16
17
18

THUNDER from the SEA

ADVENTURE ON BOARD THE HMS *DEFENDER*

JEFF WEIGEL

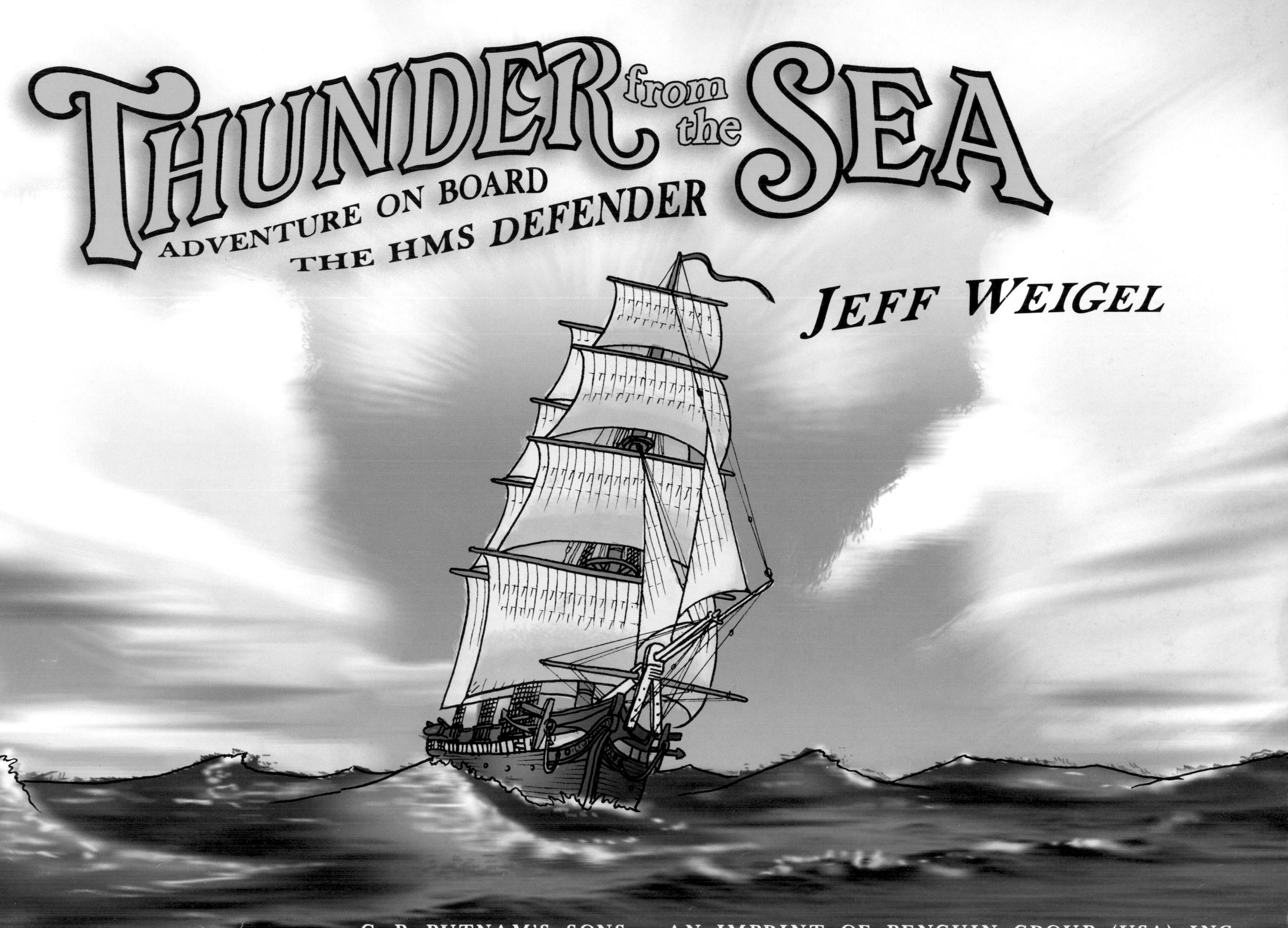

G. P. PUTNAM'S SONS • AN IMPRINT OF PENGUIN GROUP (USA) INC.

THE NAPOLEONIC WARS

In 1789, an uprising of France's citizens against King Louis XVI left the remaining monarchies of Europe stunned and threatened. Quickly, the democratic ideals of the French Revolution deteriorated into violence that threatened to spread to France's neighbors. Great Britain, Austria, Spain and Prussia soon went to war with France to crush this threat to their traditional social order, and all of Europe was quickly drawn into the conflict. In the years that followed, a French military officer named Napoleon Bonaparte rose through the ranks and led France to victory against its enemies.

Bonaparte was a general with limitless daring, unparalleled military skill, and an insatiable thirst for power. But he had more than just defending France's new democratic principles on his mind. After achieving a string of military successes, and with a loyal army at his command, Bonaparte staged a coup in 1799 that made him dictator of France, eventually crowning himself emperor and finally dashing the democratic ideals of the people's revolution. He then set out to conquer the entire continent of Europe and make it his empire.

By 1805, most of Europe had either fallen to Napoleon's army or had allied with him in an attempt to avoid his aggression. England was the only remaining obstacle to Bonaparte's ambitions. And so the British braced for what seemed inevitable—a French invasion of their country from across the English Channel. The only defense for the island nation was the might of the British Royal Navy. With England desperate to fill out the crews of undermanned warships in the nation's hour of need, the navy accepted the skilled and unskilled, the old and the young. And so, even a boy could find himself at sea, swept up in events as the future of the world hung in the balance.

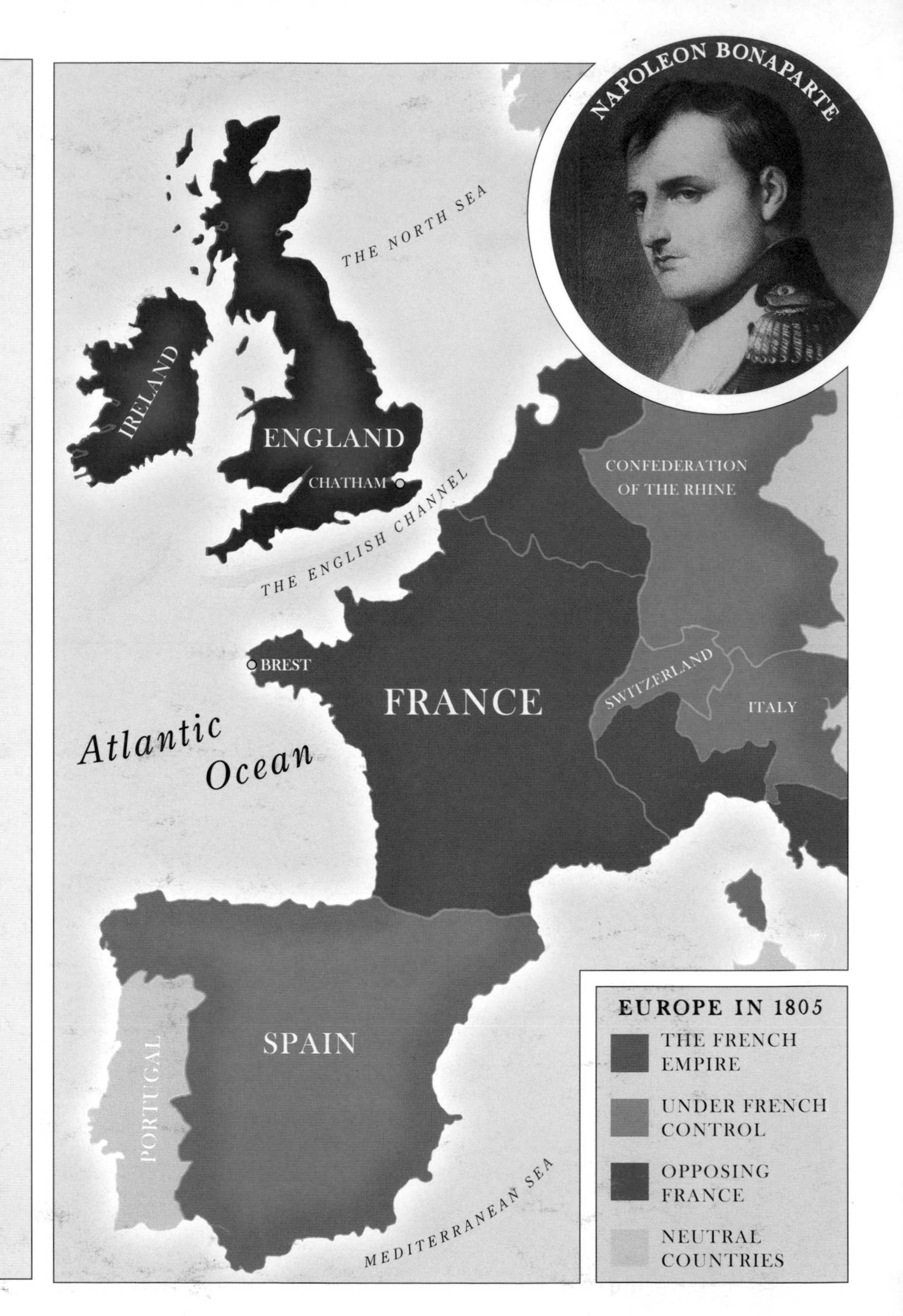

APRIL 1805—THE PORT OF CHATHAM ON THE COAST OF ENGLAND
GENTLEMEN, THIS IS JACK HOYTON— THE NEW CREWMAN ASSIGNED TO US.
THAT'S HER, LT. TREMAINE? THAT'S MY SHIP?
THAT'S HER, MR. HOYTON. YOUR NEW HOME—HMS DEFENDER.
BLIMEY, LT. TREMAINE, HE'S A BABY! CAN'T THE NAVY FIND US ANY MEN NO MORE?
GIVE 'IM A CHANCE. HE LOOKS FIT ENOUGH TO SCRUB A DECK, ANYWAY.

His Majesty's Navy
King George III was ruler of Great Britain from 1760 to 1820. All British navy ships were designated "His Majesty's Ship," or HMS.

Frigate
Frigates were fast, square-sailed ships with only a single gun deck below topside. They were used primarily as escorts or for patrol duty because of their speed and maneuverability.

Seamen and Landsmen
Experienced sailors were referred to as seamen, while new sailors were called landsmen. Landsmen were commonly used for brute work such as moving cargo and scrubbing the decks.

Bosun
A boatswain, or "bosun" for short, was a low-level officer responsible for maintaining the sails and riggings.

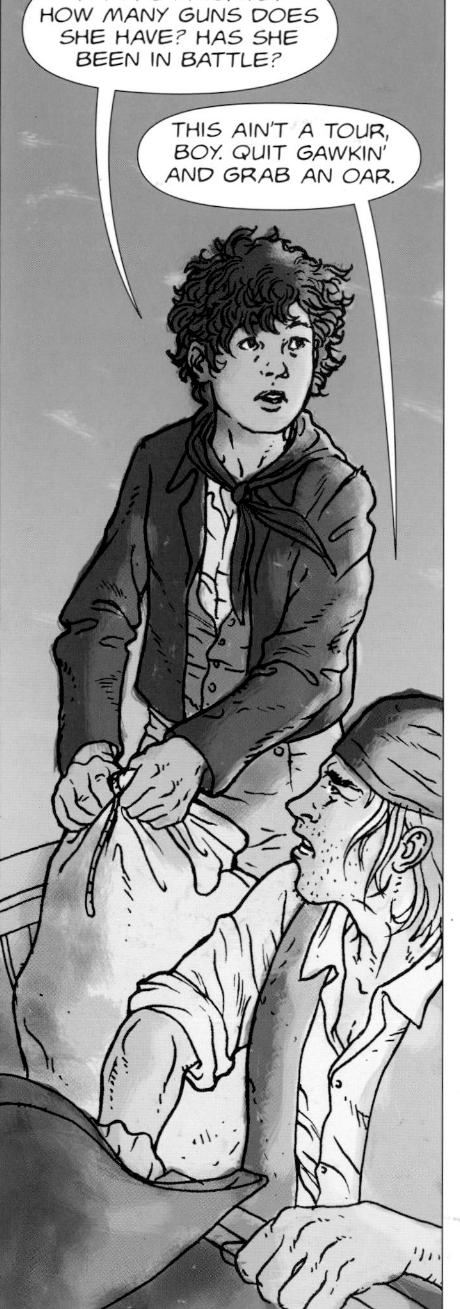

A REAL FRIGATE! HOW MANY GUNS DOES SHE HAVE? HAS SHE BEEN IN BATTLE?
THIS AIN'T A TOUR, BOY. QUIT GAWKIN' AND GRAB AN OAR.

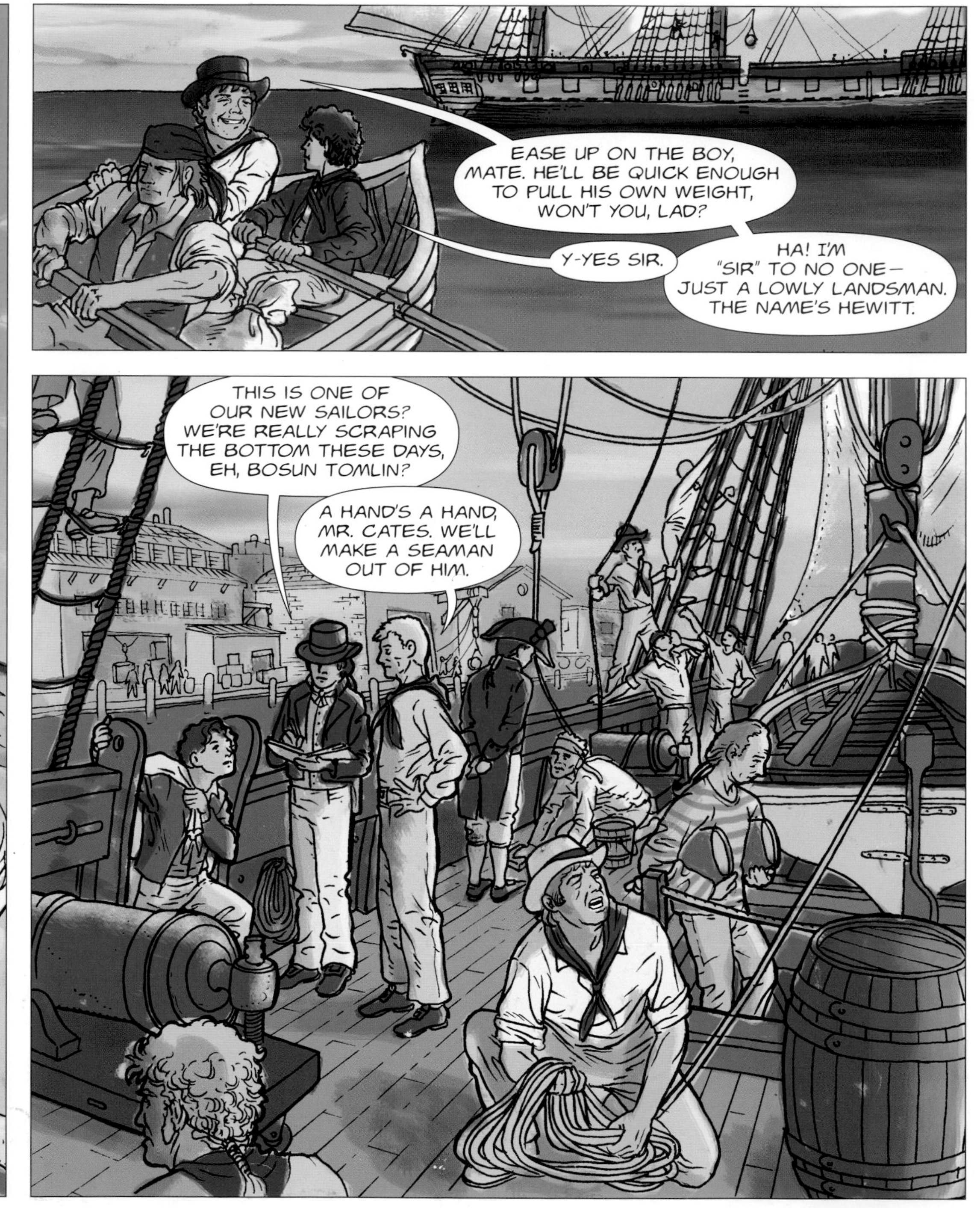

EASE UP ON THE BOY, MATE. HE'LL BE QUICK ENOUGH TO PULL HIS OWN WEIGHT, WON'T YOU, LAD?
Y-YES SIR.
HA! I'M "SIR" TO NO ONE— JUST A LOWLY LANDSMAN. THE NAME'S HEWITT.
THIS IS ONE OF OUR NEW SAILORS? WE'RE REALLY SCRAPING THE BOTTOM THESE DAYS, EH, BOSUN TOMLIN?
A HAND'S A HAND, MR. CATES. WE'LL MAKE A SEAMAN OUT OF HIM.

MIDSHIPMAN CATES, THIS IS OUR NEW BOY FROM THE MARITIME SOCIETY. ADD HIM TO THE SHIP'S MUSTER WHILE I REPORT TO THE CAPTAIN.
AYE, LT. TREMAINE. NAME AND AGE, LAD.
JACK HOYTON, SIR. I'M TWELVE.
FROM THE MARITIME SOCIETY—AN ORPHAN, THEN?
NO. I'VE A FATHER... SOMEWHERE...BUT HE WAS PRESSED INTO SERVICE WHEN I WAS SIX.
MY AUNT CARED FOR ME FOR A WHILE, BUT THE MARITIME BOYS' HOME HAS HAD ME FOR THREE YEARS AND—
YES, WELL—AS GOOD AS AN ORPHAN, THEN.
MR. HOYTON, I'M RATING YOU AS "BOY, THIRD CLASS." TOMLIN, TAKE CHARGE OF THIS LAD AND PUT HIM TO WORK.
YOUR FATHER'S A SAILOR, IS HE, MR. HOYTON? GOOD FOR HIM! I'LL DO MY BEST TO MAKE SURE YOU CAN MATCH HIM KNOT FOR KNOT AND NERVE FOR NERVE THE NEXT TIME YOU SEE HIM.
THANK YOU, SIR.
STEP BELOW. YOU CAN STOW YOUR GEAR AND THEN WE'LL SET ABOUT GETTING YOUR HANDS DIRTY.

The Maritime Society
A number of philanthropic organizations looked after orphans and waifs in English society, occasionally providing them with a career by placing them with the British navy. The navy was known to have accepted boys as young as seven, but twelve- and thirteen-year-olds were more common.

Impressment
In times of war, the British navy resorted to what amounted to kidnapping to fill out its ships' crews. Small groups of men, called press gangs, roamed the English port towns and "recruited" new sailors by force. These "pressed" recruits made up as much as two thirds of the British navy during the years of the Napoleonic conflict.

Ship's Cannons
A cannon's power and size were measured by the weight of the cannonball it was built to fire. An 18-pound ball was common for a frigate's cannons. A larger, higher-rated ship might carry guns that fired shot as heavy as 32 pounds.

Sealing the Decks
Loosely unraveled rope, called oakum, was pounded into the cracks between deck planks with special hammers and chisels; then melted pitch (a tar-like substance) was poured over the seam to seal the decks against water.

WE SLEEP AND EAT HERE ON THE GUN DECK. FIND A HOOK FOR YOUR DUFFEL, LAD.
CANNONS!
AYE. 18-POUNDERS. WE'VE GOT 38 OF 'EM, ALL TOLD. YOU'LL BE ON MY GUN CREW.
I'LL BE HELPING TO FIRE THE CANNONS?
YOU'LL DO NO SUCH THING. YOU'LL FETCH POWDER FOR US...
...AND YOU'LL TRY NOT TO GET BLOWN TO A BLOODY MIST OR CRUSHED BY A RECOIL WHILE YOU DO IT.
YOU'LL BE LESS FOND OF THE CANNONS AFTER A FEW DAYS OF GUNNERY DRILLS.
BUT IN THE MEANTIME...
LATER...
YOU'VE HAD HIM UNRAVELING ROPE ALL AFTERNOON. IS THE BOY BEING PUNISHED, MR. TOMLIN?
NO SIR. A FEW HOURS OF MAKING OAKUM FOR THE DECKS ALWAYS HELPS KNOCK ROMANTIC NOTIONS OF LIFE AT SEA OUT OF NEW BOYS.
BESIDES, HE'S GOT A LOT TO LEARN BEFORE HE'S FIT FOR MUCH ELSE.
HE MAY NOT KNOW THE MIZZENMAST FROM THE POWDER MAGAZINE NOW, BUT I'LL CHANGE THAT BEFORE WE REACH THE WATERS OFF FRANCE.

IN THE DAYS THAT FOLLOW...
I HEAR WE'RE HEADED FOR BLOCKADE DUTY NEAR BREST. THAT MEANS MONTHS OF BOREDOM, PATROLLIN' THE SHORES AND CHASIN' DOWN "FROG" SUPPLY SHIPS.
THE ADMIRALTY'S HOPING TO BOX UP THE FRENCHIES IN THEIR PORTS SO THEY CAN'T MOUNT AN INVASION OF ENGLAND.
DO YOU REALLY THINK THE FRENCH WOULD INVADE US?
BONAPARTE'D LOVE TO ADD ENGLAND TO HIS COLLECTION, BUT HE'LL HAVE TO GET PAST THE LIKES OF US BEFORE HE TAKES OUR HOMES.
AH, YOU BRITS ARE SPOILED. WE IRISH ARE USED TO INVASION. WHY, YOU'VE BEEN LORDIN' OVER US FOREVER!
BELAY THAT TALK, HEWITT. YOU AND EVERYONE ON THIS SHIP ARE BRITISH SUBJECTS. WE'VE ALL AN EQUAL STAKE IN DOING OUR DUTY TO STOP BONAPARTE.
AYE, LT. TREMAINE.
JACK AND WILLIE, YOU TWO BOYS REPORT TOPSIDE TO ASSIST MR. TOMLIN.
MOMENTS LATER...
UP TO THE MIZZEN TOPSAIL, LADS. WE'LL CLIMB OUT ON THE YARDARM AND I'LL SHOW YOU HOW TO HANG A NEW SAIL.
C'MON, JACK. I WAS SCARED MY FIRST FEW TIMES, BUT YOU GET USED TO WORKIN' UP HIGH.
IT LOOKS LIKE FUN TO ME, WILLIE!

Frogs and Limeys

The English gave their foes the derogatory nickname of "frogs" because of France's fondness for fried frogs' legs. The British navy's policy of feeding sailors limes as a way of preventing a disease called scurvy led their enemies to refer to the English as "limeys."

Mizzen Topsail

Each of the ship's three tall masts had its own name. The foremast was at the front of the ship, the mainmast was at the center, and the mizzenmast was at the stern, or rear. Each sail had a name, too. The lowest sail was the mainsail, the next above it was a topsail, the next above that was a topgallant, and the uppermost sail was a topgallant royal.

Topmen
Topmen were the sailors charged with climbing to the heights of the masts to handle the sails. This was dangerous work, but an experienced topman was considered to be among the most elite and skilled members of the crew.

Heaving on a Reef
A horizontal section along the top of a sail—called the reef—could be gathered to reduce the sail's wind exposure.

The Battle of the Nile
In 1798, a spectacular naval battle occurred between the French and the English near the mouth of the Nile River in Egypt. The decisive British victory there crippled Napoleon's navy and ended his plans for a conquest of India, his intended target to the East.

THE NEW BOY MOVES LIKE A MONKEY UP THERE. HE MAY MAKE A FINE TOPMAN.
WE'LL SEE, SIR. WE'VE NEEDED A NIMBLE NEW HAND SINCE SMYTH FELL LAST MONTH.
HEAVE ON THAT REEF, YOU TWO.
WILLIE, HOW LONG HAVE YOU BEEN ABOARD THE DEFENDER?
SIX MONTHS, BUT BEFORE THIS I SPENT A WHILE ABOARD A SLOOP.
MY FAMILY SENT ME TO SEA ON A MERCHANT SHIP SO'S I COULD LEARN A TRADE, BUT I GOT PRESSED BY THE NAVY BEFORE LONG—THEY'RE ALWAYS RAIDING CIVILIAN VESSELS FOR MORE CREW.
PRESSED OR NOT, I'M LUCKY TO BE ON THE DEFENDER. CAPTAIN MOORE'S A REAL HERO—HE WAS A LIEUTENANT ON A SHIP-OF-THE-LINE AT THE BATTLE OF THE NILE.
THE REST OF THE CREW IS A MIXED LOT—SEASONED SAILORS, TRADESMEN, MARINES. THERE'S ABOUT FIFTEEN OF US BOYS.
WHAT ARE THE OFFICERS LIKE?
THE LIEUTENANTS—TREMAINE, NEWTON AND FORBES—THEY'RE A DECENT BUNCH, AND THE MIDSHIPMEN ARE HARMLESS ENOUGH...
...EXCEPT FOR MR. CATES. HE'S THE SON OF SOME LORD. HE ACTS LIKE HE OWNS THE SHIP. STEER CLEAR OF HIM IF YOU CAN.

LATER IN THE DAY...
SO, MY LAD, HOW ARE YOU FINDING LIFE IN HIS MAJESTY'S NAVY SO FAR?
TODAY I FEEL MORE LIKE A SCRUB-WOMAN THAN A SAILOR, HEWITT.
THERE'S WORSE WORK THAN PUSHIN' A HOLYSTONE ACROSS THE DECKS. WAIT'LL YOU HAVE TO TRIM A SAIL IN A HOWLING STORM.
THE NAVY'S NO LIFE OF LEISURE, BUT YOU'LL ALWAYS HAVE A HAMMOCK TO SLEEP IN AND A FULL BELLY AT THE END OF THE DAY. THAT'S MORE THAN I HAD BACK IN IRELAND.
OR I AT THE ORPHANAGE.
'COURSE, THAT DON'T STOP ME FROM MISSIN' ME HOME.
YOU WON'T EARN ANY RATIONS AT THIS LUBBERLY PACE, MR. HEWITT.
NO MORE EXCUSES. GET BACK TO WORK.
SORRY, MR. CATES. JUST GIVING ME POOR KNEES A BREAK.
IT WAS JUST A MOMENT'S REST, SIR. SCRUBBING WITH THIS SAND AND SALT WATER HAS OUR KNEES RAW.
ENOUGH COMPLAINTS, MR. HOYTON. YOU'LL BOTH DO AS I SAY AND YOU'LL LOOK LIVELY DOING IT...
...OR I'LL REPORT YOUR SLOTH TO LIEUTENANT TREMAINE!

Holystone
Decks were cleaned by scrubbing sand over wet boards using a flat piece of sandstone called a holystone—so named because it was roughly the size of a typical prayer book, and because sailors had to get down on their knees when using it.

Lubberly
"Lubber" was a contemptuous word for an inexperienced and unskilled sailor.

Naval Blockade
Since the earliest days of organized naval warfare, the tactic of cutting off all ocean traffic from an opponent's shores has been used to starve an enemy of any resources—from food to war materials—that might be delivered by sea.

Admiral Lord Horatio Nelson
England's greatest naval hero of the Napoleonic War was Admiral Nelson. His reputation for courageous leadership and strategic thinking made him an icon of the British navy.

YOU STRAY CATS FRESH FROM THE POORHOUSE ARE ALL THE SAME. NO DISCIPLINE. HOW THE ADMIRALTY EXPECTS US TO MAINTAIN A BLOCKADE OF FRANCE WITH THE LIKES OF YOU I'LL NEVER KNOW.

HUMPF. HIGH AND MIGHTY MR. MIDSHIPMAN CATES. ALL OF SEVENTEEN AND HE THINKS HE'S LORD NELSON HIMSELF.

NO, JACK! NO...

DON'T!

MY LAD, IT APPEARS THAT YOUR HOLYSTONE WAS BOUND FOR THE HEAD OF MIDSHIPMAN CATES. IF SO, YOU MAY WISH TO THANK MR. HEWITT FOR SAVING YOUR LIFE.
YOU ARE NEW TO THE DEFENDER, ARE YOU NOT, MISTER—?
EH... THIS IS MR. HOYTON, CAPTAIN.
MR. HOYTON, NO DOUBT YOUR LIFE ON LAND HAS LED YOU TO TRADE BLOWS WITH YOUR FELLOW STREET URCHINS AT THE DROP OF A HAT.
YOU WILL FIND THE ROYAL NAVY QUITE DIFFERENT FROM THE STREETS OF LONDON.
ACCORDING TO THE ARTICLES OF WAR, THE PUNISHMENT FOR STRIKING AN OFFICER...
...IS DEATH...
...BY HANGING.
HE WAS GOING TO STRIKE ME?!
MR. TOMLIN, I THINK A DOZEN STROKES SHOULD CEMENT THIS LESSON WITH OUR NEW CHARGE. PLEASE SEE TO IT.
AYE, SIR.
MR. CATES, I OVERHEARD YOUR EXCHANGE WITH MR. HOYTON...
ONE OF THE TESTS OF A GOOD OFFICER IS THE RESPECT HIS CONDUCT AND DEMEANOR ENGENDER FROM THE MEN WHO SERVE UNDER HIM.
TODAY YOU HAVE FAILED THIS TEST.

The Royal Navy's Articles of War

The laws of conduct in the navy were defined by 34 Articles of War, a document dating from the mid-1700s. They listed forbidden conduct for sailors, and accompanying punishments.

Midshipmen

Midshipmen were non-commissioned officers in the navy who were in training to eventually become full officers. Most often, they were young boys with a few years of experience at sea.

Punishment
Punishment in the navy was swift, harsh and common. Maintaining discipline and obedience was an absolute necessity on board a fighting ship. Mutiny—the takeover of a ship by its crew—was a captain's worst fear, and the best defense against it was the threat of stern punishment for even the slightest infractions.

BUT MR. TOMLIN, I NEVER EVEN THREW THE STONE...
...AND CATES HAD IT COMING, ANYWAY!
H-HE SAID...
MAKES NO DIFFERENCE, JACK.
THE CAPTAIN'S GOING EASY ON YOU AT A DOZEN STROKES.
STEP UP TO THE CANNON.
B-BUT... IT'S NOT FAIR.
FAIR DON'T ENTER INTO IT.
I'LL MAKE THIS AS QUICK AS I CAN. OFF WITH YOUR SHIRT.
LEAN OVER THE GUN, BOY.
HOLD HIM STEADY, MR. WELLES.
WHI-CRACK
ONE...

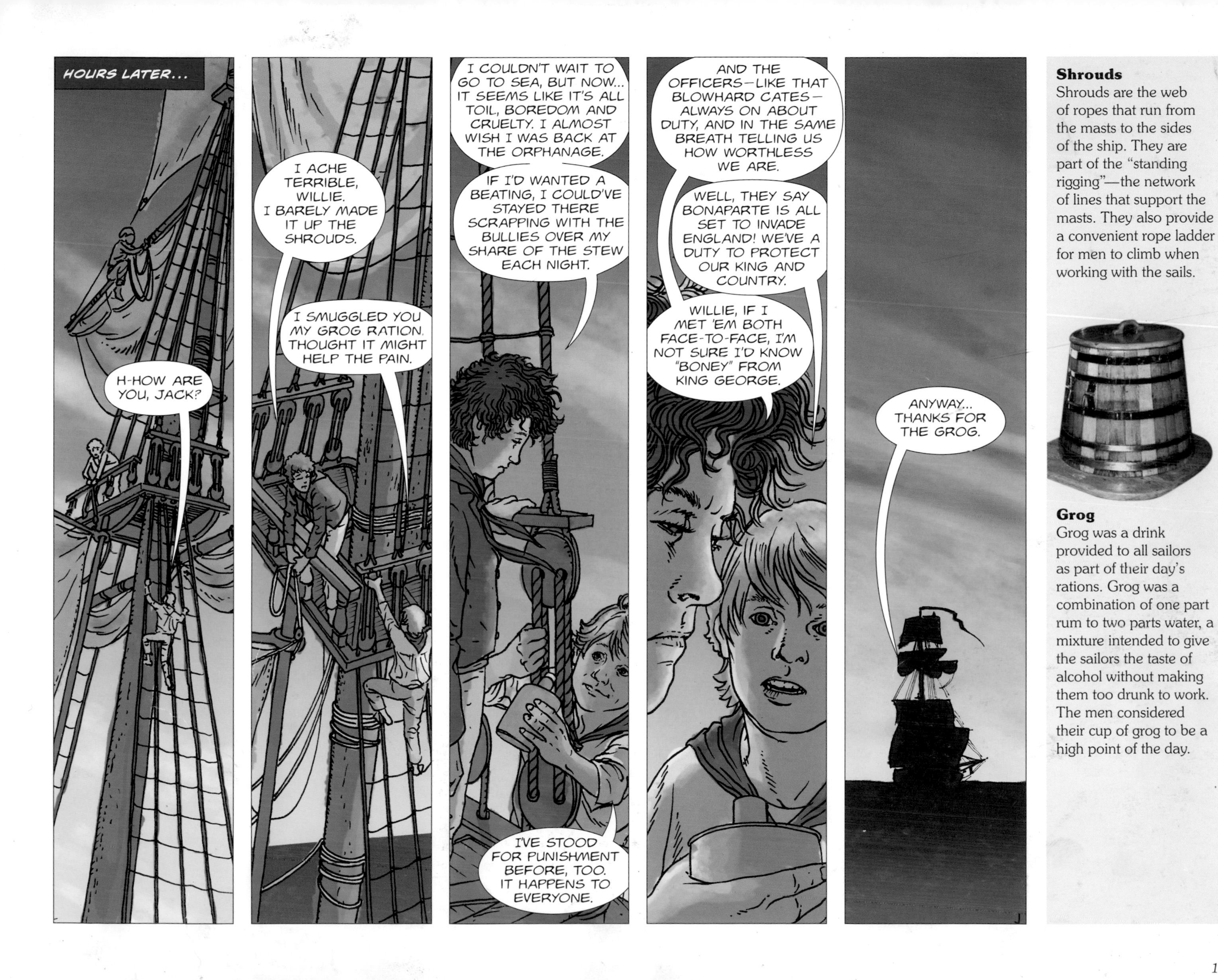
HOURS LATER...
H-HOW ARE YOU, JACK?
I ACHE TERRIBLE, WILLIE. I BARELY MADE IT UP THE SHROUDS.
I SMUGGLED YOU MY GROG RATION. THOUGHT IT MIGHT HELP THE PAIN.
I COULDN'T WAIT TO GO TO SEA, BUT NOW... IT SEEMS LIKE IT'S ALL TOIL, BOREDOM AND CRUELTY. I ALMOST WISH I WAS BACK AT THE ORPHANAGE.
IF I'D WANTED A BEATING, I COULD'VE STAYED THERE SCRAPPING WITH THE BULLIES OVER MY SHARE OF THE STEW EACH NIGHT.
I'VE STOOD FOR PUNISHMENT BEFORE, TOO. IT HAPPENS TO EVERYONE.
AND THE OFFICERS—LIKE THAT BLOWHARD CATES—ALWAYS ON ABOUT DUTY, AND IN THE SAME BREATH TELLING US HOW WORTHLESS WE ARE.
WELL, THEY SAY BONAPARTE IS ALL SET TO INVADE ENGLAND! WE'VE A DUTY TO PROTECT OUR KING AND COUNTRY.
WILLIE, IF I MET 'EM BOTH FACE-TO-FACE, I'M NOT SURE I'D KNOW "BONEY" FROM KING GEORGE.
ANYWAY... THANKS FOR THE GROG.

Shrouds
Shrouds are the web of ropes that run from the masts to the sides of the ship. They are part of the "standing rigging"—the network of lines that support the masts. They also provide a convenient rope ladder for men to climb when working with the sails.

Grog
Grog was a drink provided to all sailors as part of their day's rations. Grog was a combination of one part rum to two parts water, a mixture intended to give the sailors the taste of alcohol without making them too drunk to work. The men considered their cup of grog to be a high point of the day.

FIRE!
BOOM!
BOOM!
BOOM!
BOOM!
AFTER DAYS AT SEA, THE DEFENDER ARRIVES AT THE STRETCH OF FRENCH COASTLINE IT'S BEEN ASSIGNED TO PATROL...
GOOD WORK, MEN. THAT'S ENOUGH GUNNERY PRACTICE FOR TODAY.
I THINK WE CAN GET OUR RELOADING TIME DOWN BELOW A MINUTE AFTER A FEW MORE PRACTICES, LIEUTENANT.
TOO BAD WE CAN'T ELEVATE THE GUNS ENOUGH TO FIRE AT THE BATTERY ABOVE THE VILLAGE IN THAT COVE, SIR. WE'LL HAVE TO STAY OUT OF THEIR REACH.
THE LITTLE VILLAGE OF DUMONT IS THE LEAST OF OUR CONCERNS, TOMLIN.
YOU MAKE A FINE POWDER MONKEY, MR. HOYTON, BUT YOU LOOK EXHAUSTED.
YOU DID YOUR DUTY WELL, LAD.
AYE, SIR. IF "DUTY" MEANS RUNNING TILL MY LEGS ARE JELLY AND SWEATING LIKE A PLOW HORSE!
I DON'T THINK HE KNOWS QUITE WHAT TO MAKE OF LIFE AT SEA.
GIVE HIM TIME. HE'LL COME AROUND.

Powder Monkey
Loading and arming a cannon required a small crew of men. Since storing gunpowder near the firing cannons was too hazardous, young boys nicknamed "powder monkeys" raced to the lower decks where the gunpowder was stored and brought individual charges up to the gun crew. It was dangerous work since a spill and a stray spark could mean instant disaster!

DAYS TURN INTO WEEKS AS THE DEFENDER PATROLS THE FRENCH COASTLINE.
OFF STARBOARD, SIR! A MERCHANT SCHOONER TRYING TO RACE PAST US INTO DUMONT.
HAUL TO THE WIND, LT. TREMAINE. WE'LL SEE IF WE CAN CATCH HER.
BOOM!
SPLOOSH
A CANNONBALL! WE'VE STRAYED TOO CLOSE TO THE BATTERY ATOP THE CLIFFS!
BREAK OFF THE CHASE!
I'M GROWING TIRED OF THOSE INFERNAL GUNS FOILING OUR EFFORTS TO BLOCKADE THAT VILLAGE.
WE CAN'T EVEN GET CLOSE ENOUGH TO SEE INTO THE COVE. WHAT COULD THEY BE GUARDING SO JEALOUSLY IN THAT TOWN?
SIR, THE PURSER REPORTS OUR SUPPLY OF DRINKING WATER GROWS STALE. WE'LL NEED TO REPLENISH IT SOON.
VERY WELL. WE'LL SAIL TO A SECLUDED SPOT AND YOU CAN TAKE A GROUP ASHORE TO FIND FRESH WATER.
YOU HEAR THAT, JACK?
I'D VOLUNTEER TO GO ASHORE JUST TO FEEL GRASS UNDER MY FEET AGAIN.

Starboard
The right side of a vessel as one stands on deck facing the front, or bow, is called starboard. The left side is port.

Schooner
A schooner is a light, speedy vessel built to run with at least two front and back sails that hang at angles to the body of the ship. A small craft like a schooner would be nimble quarry for a frigate.

Shipboard Rations
Since ships were separated from their home ports for long stretches of time, they carried large stores of food and water to sustain the crew. But without modern refrigeration and sanitary storage methods, supplies grew stale over time. To replenish their stocks, ships relied on the occasional rendezvous with the fleet's supply vessels, a stop in a friendly port, or even a trip to shore to hunt for wild game and fresh springwater.

CARE TO STAND ON SOLID EARTH AGAIN, MR. HOYTON?
YES SIR!
THE DEFENDER SAILS TO A DESERTED STRETCH OF COAST AND THEN...
KEEP TOGETHER, MEN. WE'LL FILL OUR KEGS AT THE WATERFALL OVER THERE.
IT FEELS STRANGE TO BE ON FRENCH SOIL.
WE'RE SAFE ENOUGH, I'LL WAGER. WE'RE MILES FROM ANY VILLAGE.
STILL, HEWITT, THERE COULD BE FRENCH PATROLS MOVING THROUGH THE AREA. STAY ALERT.
TREES AND GRASS ARE A WELCOME CHANGE OF SCENERY!
CRACK!
UUGH!
WHA—! WE'VE BEEN SPOTTED!
MARINES TO THE FORE! RETURN FIRE!
CRACK!
CRACK!
MORE SHOTS FROM THE RIGHT, SIR!
CRACK!
UUH!

PRIVATE SIMMS IS DEAD!
AND MORE ARE WOUNDED! WE'RE BEING SLAUGHTERED HERE! RETREAT TO THE LONGBOAT!
WH-WHERE'S HEWITT?!
HEWITT'S MISSING!
WE CAN'T WAIT FOR HIM! IF WE DON'T PUSH OFF NOW, WE'LL ALL BE LOST!
ROW, MEN! PUT YOUR BACKS INTO IT!
THWIIP
THWIIP
THWIIP
WE'RE OUT OF RANGE NOW. WE'VE GOT TO GET THE WOUNDED BACK TO THE SHIP.
BUT...BUT HEWITT'S STILL BACK THERE! CAN'T WE HELP HIM SOMEHOW?
I SAW HEWITT RUN OFF INTO THE WOODS, SIR.
WE... CAN'T JUST ABANDON...
HEWITT MUST'VE PANICKED. WE COULDN'T WAIT FOR HIM, LAD, OR WE'D SURELY ALL BE FRENCH PRISONERS.

Marines
Starting in 1804, every British naval vessel carried a contingent of Royal Marines. They accounted for as much as one fifth of the crew. They served as the ship's main fighting force, and as guardians against mutiny by the sailors. Their red coats earned them the nickname "lobsters."

Sleeping Quarters
Space was very limited on naval vessels and no room could be spared for luxuries like bunks. Men on frigates like the *Defender* slept on the gun deck in hammocks. They were hung a regulation 14 inches apart, which made for shoulder-to-shoulder conditions that saved space and also prevented too much swaying when the ship encountered rough seas.

BACK ON THE SHIP, AS EVENING FALLS...
YOU WAS LUCKY TO MAKE IT BACK FROM SHORE IN ONE PIECE, JACK. JOHNSTON'S WOUND WAS SO BAD THE SURGEON HAD TO TAKE HIS ARM OFF AT THE SHOULDER.
AND A MARINE DEAD, TOO!
I FEEL LIKE A COWARD, WILLIE. MY ONLY THOUGHT WAS TO RUN—EVEN BEFORE THE LIEUTENANT ORDERED US TO RETREAT.
AND THEN WE LEFT POOR HEWITT BEHIND!
MAYBE HE GOT AWAY AND FOUND A SAFE HIDING PLACE.
JUST BE GLAD YOU MADE IT BACK SAFE AND SOUND!
JACK, YOU NEED A LUCKY CHARM LIKE THE REST OF US CARRY, FOR WHEN THE SHOT STARTS TO FLY.
LUCKY CHARM?
SURE! I KEEPS THIS LETTER FROM ME WIFE. I'M AS SAFE AS THE CROWN JEWELS WITH THIS IN ME POCKET.
I HAVE SOMETHING MY FATHER GAVE ME WHEN I WAS LITTLE...
...THIS MAGNIFYING GLASS I WEAR AROUND MY NECK.
DO YOU THINK IT COULD BE LUCKY?
DON'T MIND THAT RUBBISH, BOY. YOUR BEST DEFENSE IS TO KEEP YOUR WITS ABOUT YOU AND FOLLOW ORDERS.
...AND JACK, I'LL WAGER YOU WEREN'T ANY MORE AFRAID THAN THE REST OF THOSE MEN TODAY.
NOW OFF TO SLEEP WITH' YOU.

SEVERAL DAYS LATER...
A BOAT'S APPROACHING FROM STARBOARD.
PROBABLY A LOCAL FISHERMAN LOOKING TO SELL US HIS CATCH.
IF ANY FRENCH SOLDIERS SPY HIM TRADING WITH US, THEY'LL STRING HIM UP.
THAT'S HIS PROBLEM, MR. HOYTON. GO FETCH THE PURSER TO DEAL WITH THIS FELLOW.
WHAT THE DEVIL? HE'S GOT NO FISH TO SELL! THEN WHAT COULD HE BE...
IT'S HEWITT!
AHOY, DEFENDER!
HEWITT! WE'D GIVEN YOU UP FOR LOST!
NEVER GIVE UP ON THE IRISH, JACK. WE COULD BEAT THE DEVIL AT DICE!
I SLIPPED AWAY FROM THOSE FROGS THAT ATTACKED US. THEN I "BORROWED" THIS BOAT FROM A LOCAL FELLA WHO'S NOW SPORTIN' A KNOT ON HIS NOGGIN.
I'VE GOT URGENT NEWS FOR THE CAPTAIN.
MOMENTS LATER...
YOU CLAIM THE BATTERY CAN BE TAKEN, MR. HEWITT?
AYE, SIR. THAT FIRST NIGHT I TOOK COVER IN A HOLLOW TREE AND THE SOLDIERS MADE CAMP A STONE'S THROW AWAY. MY FRENCH IS GOOD ENOUGH TO HEAR 'EM JABBERIN'. THEY SAID THERE'S NOTHIN' BUT A HANDFUL OF MEN IN THAT OLD FORT.
ACCORDING TO THE FROGS, THERE'S NO MORE THAN TWENTY MEN WORKING THOSE GUNS.

Purser
The purser was in charge of all the ship's food, clothing and provisions. He kept inventory and dealt with the purchase of supplies whenever the ship was in port or when he had the opportunity to replenish stores by trading with those on land. He was often resented by the men on board because of the assumption that his position gave him a greater share of the ship's provisions.

The Captain's Quarters

The captain was the only man on a frigate to enjoy the privacy of a room to himself, although he did share it with the cannons at the aft of the ship. His stateroom also served as a meeting room for the officers to gather and plan. A marine always stood guard outside the captain's quarters to repel any attempt at mutiny.

SHORTLY AFTER, THE OFFICERS GATHER IN THE CAPTAIN'S QUARTERS TO DEBATE AND PLAN...
...UNTIL FINALLY...
BOSUN TOMLIN, ASSEMBLE THE MEN.
ALL HANDS ON DECK!
FOR LONG WEEKS NOW, WE'VE WANDERED AIMLESSLY IN THIS FORSAKEN BACKWATER OF THE WAR. OUR EVERY EFFORT TO FULFILL OUR MISSION HERE HAS BEEN CUT SHORT BY THE GUNS ABOVE DUMONT.
NO LONGER! NOW WE TAKE THE FIGHT TO THE FRENCH!
THIS EVENING, LIEUTENANTS NEWTON AND TREMAINE WILL LEAD A RAIDING PARTY GUIDED BY MR. HEWITT. THEY WILL CAPTURE THE BATTERY WITH AS MUCH STEALTH AS THEY CAN MANAGE.
ONCE THE FORT IS OURS, THE DEFENDER SHALL ENTER DUMONT AND END ITS CONTRIBUTION TO NAPOLEON'S WAR EFFORT.
YOU MEN HAVE LONGED FOR DUTY MORE EXCITING THAN SCRUBBING DECKS AND FOLDING SAILS. YOU'RE ABOUT TO GET IT.
HURRAH!
JACK, YOU'RE TO REPORT TO LT. TREMAINE.
BUT ISN'T HE BUSY ORGANIZING THE RAID?
AYE. YOU'RE GOING ASHORE TONIGHT WITH THE RAIDING PARTY.

YOU THIRTY MEN WILL BE GOING ASHORE WITH LT. NEWTON AND ME. OUR MISSION IS TO TAKE THE GUN BATTERY BY SURPRISE AND CAPTURE IT. BY MR. HEWITT'S ACCOUNT, WE'LL BE UP AGAINST FEWER THAN TWENTY FRENCH SOLDIERS.
ONCE WE SECURE OUR TARGET, MR. HEWITT AND MR. HOYTON WILL RETURN TO SHORE TO SIGNAL OUR SUCCESS TO THE DEFENDER BY RAISING SAIL FROM THEIR FISHING BOAT.
SIR, IS IT WISE TO ENTRUST SUCH AN IMPORTANT TASK TO THIS... BOY?
HEWITT AND JACK WILL BE DISGUISED AS A FISHERMAN AND HIS SON SETTING OFF TO WORK. THE YOUNGER THE BOY, THE MORE CONVINCING THE RUSE.
YOU CAN COUNT ON ME, SIR.
NOW, MR. CATES, TAKE OUR TWO SPIES BELOW AND SEE THAT THEY'RE PREPARED FOR THEIR MISSION.
I HAVE SINCERE DOUBTS ABOUT THE WISDOM OF CHOOSING YOU FOR THIS TASK, BUT IT APPEARS WE MUST MAKE THE MOST OF OUR LIMITED RESOURCES.
I'LL DO MY DUTY JUST FINE! JUST AS WELL AS YOU...SIR!
SEE THAT YOU DO, SEAMAN. MEN'S LIVES WILL BE DEPENDING ON YOU.
THOSE HATS AND OILSKIN COATS WILL MAKE YOU LOOK ENOUGH LIKE FISHERMEN.
YOU'LL NEED A COUPLE OTHER ITEMS IN CASE YOU RUN INTO MORE THAN JUST FISH.
IMAGINE, HEWITT—US AS SPIES!
ER...YEAH. IMAGINE THAT.
HERE.
AH! I SEE THE REALITY OF YOUR SITUATION HAS FINALLY DAWNED ON YOU.

Oilskin
Oilskin was a fabric used to make rain gear for sailors. It was usually sail cloth waterproofed with tar or linseed oil. Although more high-tech fabrics are used today, fishermen's waterproof clothing is still referred to as oilskins.

Naval Weapons
Rather than lances and long swords, sailors favored the tomahawk, also known as the boarding ax. It could be used in tight quarters, it was easily extracted from the body of an enemy, and the spiked end could be driven into the hull of a ship to supply a hand grip or makeshift step for climbing. The flintlock pistol was also common, but between its short, smooth-bore barrel and the rolling deck a sailor shot from, its accuracy was less than reliable. Also, it held only one shot, and the elaborate reloading process was frequently impossible in the midst of battle.

LATER, UNDER COVER OF DARKNESS, THE RAIDING PARTY SILENTLY SETS FORTH...
YOU'VE BEEN IN THESE WOODS BEFORE, HEWITT. WHICH WAY DO WE GO?
THIS WAY, SIR.
STAY CLOSE, YOU TWO. I'LL SEE TO IT YOU STAY SAFE FOR YOUR PART IN THIS MISSION.
AYE, SIR.

Phweet
HEWITT!
HEWITT, YOU BLOODY FOOL! WHAT ARE YOU DOING?
IT'S AN AMBUSH! WE'VE BEEN BETRAYED!
BY GOD! WE'LL GIVE THEM A FIGHT... UUGH!
YOU ARE SURROUNDED, MONSIEUR. DO NOT WASTE YOUR MEN'S LIVES WITH VAIN BRAVERY.
I SEEM TO HAVE LITTLE CHOICE.
MY SWORD, CAPTAIN.
WHAT DID THEY PROMISE YOU IN RETURN FOR LEADING US HERE, HEWITT—THIRTY PIECES OF SILVER?

Bosun's Pipe
A whistle called a bosun's pipe was used as a signaling device on navy ships. Its high pitch could be easily heard over the noise of a crew at work or in the din of bad weather.

Press Gangs
The gangs that scoured British villages for men to fill out the navy's ships were notoriously brutal and indiscriminate. It wasn't uncommon for them to bludgeon their reluctant recruits and whisk them from their homes and families without a moment's notice—all with the approval of the British government.

FAR MORE THAN THAT!
WHEN I WAS CAPTURED BY THE FRENCHIES, HERE, THEY THREATENED TO HANG ME AS A SPY! WELL, I HAD A BETTER IDEA FOR THEM...
I TOLD THEM I COULD ARRANGE TO DELIVER YOU LOT RIGHT INTO THEIR HANDS. SO WE MADE A DEAL—MY NECK FOR YOURS.
BUT YOU DIDN'T HAVE TO GO THROUGH WITH IT ONCE YOU GOT BACK TO THE SHIP! YOU WERE FREE!
YOU HAVEN'T HEARD THE WHOLE DEAL, JACK.
I DELIVER YOU ALL TO THE FRENCH, AND THEY DELIVER A SACK OF GOLD AND SAFE PASSAGE BACK TO IRELAND FOR ME.
THAT SOUNDED BETTER THAN MORE YEARS OF HARD TOIL AND BEATINGS FROM THESE BRITISH.
THEIR PRESS GANG DRAGGED ME FROM A WIFE AND THREE CHILDREN BACK IN IRELAND! THEY CALL ME A SAILOR, BUT I'M NO MORE THAN A SLAVE BY MY RECKONIN'!
I DON'T OWE A THING TO ANYONE ON THE DEFENDER! I JUST WANT TO GO HOME, AND NOW I'LL DO IT IN LORDLY STYLE!
ENOUGH! YOUR JOB IS NOT YET COMPLETE, MONSIEUR. WHILE WE MARCH THESE PRISONERS BACK TO OUR BATTERY'S PRISON, YOU MUST RETURN TO YOUR FISHING BOAT...
...TO GIVE THE SIGNAL THAT WILL DRAW THE BRITISH SHIP WITHIN RANGE OF OUR GUNS...
...SO THAT WE MAY BLOW IT FROM THE WATER.

HOURS LATER, IN THE FRENCH BATTERY'S PRISON...
MORNING CAN'T BE MORE THAN AN HOUR AWAY, AND THEN HEWITT WILL SIGNAL THE DEFENDER TO ITS DOOM!
BLOODY HEWITT! IF OUR PATHS EVER CROSS AGAIN, I'LL...
FORGET HEWITT. OUR IMMEDIATE CONCERN IS GETTING WORD TO THE SHIP TO STAY AWAY FROM THIS BATTERY.
BUT HOW WE'LL DO THAT FROM HERE I HAVEN'T FIGURED JUST YET.
SIR...
I THINK I CAN FIT THROUGH THE WINDOW, SIR!
WHAT'S THAT, MR. HOYTON?
BUT IT'S A SHEER WALL OUTSIDE, WITH A ROCK CLIFF BELOW THAT!
HE MIGHT FIT AT THAT!
WE CAN MAKE A ROPE FROM OUR CLOTHES. IF I REACH THE BOTTOM OF THE WALL I MIGHT MAKE IT DOWN THE CLIFFS. I'M A GOOD CLIMBER!
I'LL HEAD TO THE BEACH! I'LL FIND A WAY TO SIGNAL THE SHIP! I'LL...I'LL...
YOU APPEAR TO BE OUR ONLY HOPE, LAD.

Prisoners of War

Military men unlucky enough to be captured in the Napoleonic Wars would be locked away for the duration of the conflict. While conditions for prisoners were poor at best, they could expect to be kept alive by the enemy. Those captured as spies, however, would meet a harsher fate: the firing squad or the guillotine!

Salute
The British naval hand salute of the 1800s was a gesture of respect that consisted of a straight hand brought up to touch the brim of the hat. The palm of the hand was turned inward so the back of the hand was visible to the viewer. This was because the sailor's hand was usually stained black from working with the tarred ropes used for the ship's riggings.

LATER...
HEWITT WON'T SET OUT UNTIL THE SUN IS UP. CATCH UP WITH HIM, BUT DON'T BE FOOLISH AND TRY TO FIGHT—YOU'RE NO MATCH FOR HIM.
SEE IF YOU CAN DISABLE HIS BOAT. TRY SMASHING A HOLE IN THE HULL OR WHATEVER YOU CAN MANAGE TO STOP HIM FROM SIGNALING THE SHIP.
THIS IS YOUR CHANCE TO PROVE ME WRONG ABOUT YOU, MR. HOYTON. THE BEST OF LUCK.
THANK YOU...SIR.
UUUUGH!
YOU'RE A TIGHT FIT, LAD.
JUST KEEP PUSHING. I-I CAN MAKE IT.
GODSPEED, BOY!

GOT TO EDGE ALONG THE WALL...LOOK FOR A SPOT LESS STEEP.

I CAN'T MAKE IT DOWN THESE CLIFFS. I'M TRAPPED OUT HERE!
IF I GO BACK INSIDE I COULD BE RECAPTURED... BUT I'M NO GOOD TO ANYONE IF I STAY STUCK ON THIS LEDGE.
THE FRENCH SOLDIERS ARE PREPARING THE CANNONS...FOR WHEN THE DEFENDER COMES INTO RANGE!
I'LL NEVER MAKE IT TO THE GATE, MUCH LESS OUTSIDE TO FREEDOM...
...BUT I CAN'T JUST HIDE HERE FOREVER LIKE A RAT IN THE SHIP'S HOLD!
THE SUN'S ALMOST UP...AND THE DEFENDER COMES CLOSER TO DESTRUCTION WITH EACH MOMENT I WASTE!

France's Army

France was the first country in modern times to adopt a policy of almost universal conscription: enlisting virtually every citizen in its war effort. In 1793, a decree dubbed *levée en masse* called for all unmarried males between 18 and 25 to make themselves available for immediate military service. Married males were expected to contribute by working in fields related to the war effort, such as arms manufacturing and food production. Women were expected to sew tents and uniforms. It was this enlistment of all of France's citizens that made the French army so formidable.

Gunpowder Storage
The danger of accidental explosion was ever-present, so gunpowder was stored far away from the cannons or anything else that might generate a stray spark. On land, separate buildings called powder magazines were used. These were frequently built of stone to help contain any accidental explosion. The entrance usually faced away from the ocean and the direction of most oncoming weather, which might dampen the powder.

AS THE SECONDS TICK BY...
THE SUN'S UP. I CAN MAKE OUT THE DEFENDER OFF TOWARD THE HORIZON...
...AND THERE'S A FISHING BOAT JUST OFF THE COAST! IT'S RAISING A SAIL!
IT MUST BE HEWITT! JACK FAILED TO STOP HIM!
THE DEFENDER'S UNFURLING HER SAILS.
THEY MUST'VE SEEN HEWITT'S SIGNAL! THEY THINK WE'VE SUCCEEDED IN TAKING THE FORT!
THEY'LL SAIL RIGHT INTO THE BATTERY'S CANNON FIRE!
LIEUTENANT, NOW THAT DAYLIGHT'S BROKEN, WE CAN GET OUR FIRST GLIMPSE OF DUMONT THROUGH THIS FAR WINDOW.
YOU...YOU'D BEST COME SEE FOR YOURSELF, SIR.
GREAT GOD! THAT'S NO FISHING VILLAGE!
MORE THAN JUST THE DEFENDER IS AT STAKE HERE. IT SEEMS THE FATE OF ALL ENGLAND RESTS JUST BEYOND OUR REACH!

MEANWHILE...
SNIFF I THINK I SMELL... SNIFF
...GUNPOWDER!
THIS IS THE POWDER MAGAZINE FOR THE BATTERY!
THERE'S LOOSE POWDER EVERYWHERE! A CARELESS SPARK COULD...
THAT'S IT! AND I'VE GOT SOMETHING JUST AS GOOD AS A CARELESS SPARK!
THIS FINE TRICK ALMOST GOT ME EXPELLED FROM THE ORPHANAGE ONCE. WE'LL SEE IF THE FRENCH LIKE IT ANY BETTER.
VOUS! ARRÊTEZ-VOUS!
ARRÊTEZ-VOUS OU JE TIRE!

Magnifying Glass
A convex lens is designed to bend light to magnify an image, but this same property also enables it to focus the sunlight that passes through it into a single point. When the lens is held at the correct angle and distance from its target, the sun's concentrated rays are strong enough to start a fire in a matter of seconds.

THE WALL IS BREACHED!
THE SMOKE IS PERFECT COVER! IT'S NOW OR NEVER.
I'VE GOT TO FIND A WAY TO STOP HEWITT!

MEANWHILE, ON THE DEFENDER...
AN EXPLOSION FROM THE BATTERY! IT MUST HAVE BEEN THE POWDER MAGAZINE.
SOMETHING'S GONE AMISS! NOW THE VILLAGE WILL BE ON THE ALERT!
WHAT IN GOD'S NAME GOES ON UP THERE?
SHALL WE PROCEED, SIR?
WE HAVE LITTLE CHOICE. WE'RE FAR ENOUGH INTO THIS NARROW CHANNEL THAT WE COULDN'T TAKE THE SHIP ABOUT EVEN IF WE WANTED.
FOR GOOD OR ILL, THE DEFENDER WILL MAKE ITS STAND IN DUMONT.
LT. FORBES, BEAT TO QUARTERS!
AND IN THE PRISON...
THAT BLAST ROCKED THE WHOLE FORT!
WE'RE LUCKY THESE OLD STONE WALLS DIDN'T COME DOWN ON OUR HEADS!
WE'RE LUCKIER THAN YOU REALIZE, SIMMONS! THE WALLS ARE FRACTURED!
C'MON, MEN! YOU'VE PUT YOUR MUSCLE BEHIND A CAPSTAN OFTEN ENOUGH THAT THIS BROKEN-DOWN PRISON SHOULD BE NO MATCH FOR US.

Beat to Quarters

A beat to quarters was an alert to summon the crew to its battle stations and prepare for action. The alert was sounded by a drum being beaten to the rhythm of the official song of the British navy, a march called *Heart of Oak*.

Capstan

Pulling up the heavy anchor of a ship, plus its water-soaked cable, was accomplished by reeling it off the ocean floor with the capstan—a giant wheel turned by the sheer brute force of crewmen pushing together.

HEAVE, MEN!
HEAVE!
URRGH!
IT'S GIVIN' WAY!
WE'RE OUT! NOW SURPRISE IS ON OUR SIDE...
...HAVE AT THEM, SONS OF ENGLAND!

EVEN WITH THE MAGAZINE GONE, THERE WAS PLENTY OF GUNPOWDER IN OTHER SPOTS AROUND THE BATTERY—THEIR GUNS CAN STILL MAKE SHORT WORK OF THE DEFENDER.
IT'S HEWITT! HE MUST'VE ALREADY SENT THE SIGNAL. I'M TOO LATE!
AHOY! JACK, IS THAT YOU?
YOU ESCAPED! IT DOES ME HEART GOOD TO SEE YOU FREE, LAD. I FELT BAD ABOUT YOU SHARING THE SAME FATE AS THE OTHERS.
WHAT DO YOU KNOW ABOUT THAT EXPLOSION?
I DID THAT. I SET FIRE TO THEIR POWDER STORES.
DAMN! NOW YOU'VE COOKED MY GOOSE! THE FROGS'LL FIND A WAY TO BLAME ME FOR YOUR ACTIONS, FOR SURE!
I DON'T DARE GO BACK TO COLLECT ME MONEY. BOTH THE FRENCH AND ENGLISH'LL BE LOOKIN' TO STRING ME FROM A YARDARM!
I SHOULD FLAY YO FOR RUINING ME GOOD FORTUNE...BUT I GUE S I CAN'T HOLD A GRUDGE AGAINST YOU FOR 'IN' TO SAVE YOUR SKIN.
C'MON, LAD. NO HARD FEELIN'S. WE'LL TAKE TO THE COUNTRYSIDE AND SEE IF WE CAN'T SLIP AWAY FROM THIS MESS WITHOUT BEIN' FITTED FOR A PAIR OF NOOSES.
NO!

Hanging from the Yardarm

A common means of execution for traitors on board a ship was to be bound hand and foot and hanged by the neck from a yardarm—one of the horizontal beams from which the sails were suspended.

England and Ireland
England had controlled Ireland for more than a century when the French Revolution stirred a desire by common folk all across Europe to cast off monarchy and become democratic. In 1798, a rebellion by Irish factions longing to shed British rule was harshly put down by the English. During the Napoleonic War era, the conflict between Ireland and England was still a contentious issue, which the French tried to exploit whenever possible.

I'M NOT GOING ANYWHERE WITH YOU. YOU'RE A TRAITOR! YOU GAVE OUR LANDING PARTY UP TO THE FRENCH AND NOW YOU'VE SENT THE DEFENDER AND EVERY MAN ABOARD INTO THE HANDS OF THE ENEMY AS WELL!
AND I THOUGHT YOU WERE MY FRIEND!
I AM YOUR FRIEND! I'M OFFERING TO HELP YOU GET AWAY FROM HERE, AREN'T I?
I AIN'T PROUD OF WHAT I DONE, JACK, BUT I AIN'T SORRY NEITHER. I WAS AS GOOD AS KIDNAPPED BY THE BRITISH NAVY, AND ME HOME HAS BEEN UNDER ENGLAND'S BOOT HEEL AS LONG AS I CAN REMEMBER. YOU AND I, WE DON'T OWE KING GEORGE A THING!
MAYBE SO, BUT WHAT ABOUT THE MEN ON THE DEFENDER? WHAT ABOUT WILLIE...AND TOMLIN... AND POOR LT. NEWTON'S DEAD BECAUSE OF YOU!
BETTER HIM THAN ME, MATE.
WAIT. WHERE ARE YOU OFF TO?
I'M GOING TO JOIN MY MATES. MY REAL MATES!
GO ON AND SAVE YOUR OWN HIDE. I CAN'T STOP YOU ANYWAY.
I DON'T KNOW IF I CAN CATCH THE DEFENDER BEFORE IT'S TOO LATE, BUT I'M GOING TO TRY.
I CAN'T LET YOU DO THAT, JACK.
THE DEFENDER DON'T KNOW WHAT I DONE YET, AND I'D JUST AS SOON KEEP IT THAT WAY.

CRACK
THWIP
WHAT THE...?
FRENCH SOLDIERS!
STAY BACK, YOU BLOODY FROGS!

CRACK
AUUGH!

SPLOOSH

ARRÊTEZ LE GARÇON!

CRACK
A MISS! I'VE GOT TO ROW LIKE MAD, BEFORE THEY CAN RELOAD!

Flintlock Musket

The modern aerodynamic bullet was yet to be invented in 1805, and the flintlock musket was the standard firearm. It was loaded and fired in much the same manner as the cannon: a charge of gunpowder, a bit of cloth packing, and a round lead ball were rammed down the barrel. They were fired when the pull of the trigger released a mechanism that struck a spark, igniting the gunpowder in the barrel. Flintlocks were far less accurate than today's rifles.

Man-of-War
Large two- or three-deck naval vessels designed for direct battle with the enemy gained the nickname "man-of-war" due to their sheer size and firepower. A frigate's smaller, fewer guns and its thinner hull were considered to be no match for a man-of-war.

I'M OUT OF RANGE! NOW IF I CAN CATCH UP WITH THE DEFENDER...
THEY'RE ABOUT TO ROUND THE CLIFFS. ROW! ROW! ROW!
BOAT APPROACHING, SIR. IT LOOKS LIKE YOUNG HOYTON!
MR. HOYTON! HAUL TO SO WE CAN BRING HIM ABOARD.
WHAT THE BLAZES ARE YOU DOING HERE, LAD?!
THE CAPTAIN...! PUFF...PUFF...
...I NEED TO SEE THE CAPTAIN!
IT'S A TRAP, SIR! ...PUFF... YOU'RE BEING LURED INTO THE PORT...PUFF...SO THE BATTERY CAN FIRE ON YOU!
SIR, WE'RE ROUNDING THE CORNER! WE CAN SEE DUMONT! LOOK!
GOOD LORD!
FISHING VILLAGE... IN A PIG'S EYE!

IT'S A SHIPYARD! THEY'RE BUILDING TROOP TRANSPORTS!
AN OPERATION OF THIS SIZE CAN ONLY BE FOR ONE PURPOSE! WE'VE STUMBLED INTO PREPARATIONS FOR THE ***FRENCH INVASION OF ENGLAND!***
BOOM!
ZZZZROOMF!
A CANNONBALL! THE BATTERY'S OPENED FIRE!
NO! IT CAME FROM THE OPPOSITE DIRECTION... OVER THERE!
DEFENDER
HIDING IN THE COVE—IT'S A FRENCH ***MAN-OF-WAR!***

Ships of the Line
Naval vessels of the early 19th century varied widely in size and firepower. They were categorized by ratings based on their size and the number of guns on board. Large ships with two or three gun decks and up to 100 cannons and 850 men were rated from first- to fourth-rate. These large ships carried enough firepower to warrant sailing together in a line as the main force in a battle, and thus were referred to as "ships of the line."

OUR TINY FRIGATE AGAINST A SHIP OF THE LINE! WE'RE ALL BUT LOST!
BELAY THAT TALK, MAN!
WE HAVEN'T MUCH CHANCE IN A DIRECT BATTLE AGAINST THAT MONSTER, BUT WE'VE GOT SPEED ON OUR SIDE.
IF WE CAN RUN AROUND HER OUT TO OPEN SEAS, WE MIGHT OUTRUN HER BACK TO THE FLEET NEAR BREST WITH NEWS OF THIS SHIPYARD!
BUT BEFORE THAT WE'RE BOUND TO TAKE AT LEAST ONE BROADSIDE ATTACK FROM HER. PREPARE FOR ACTION!
YOU KNOW YOUR JOB, LAD. NOW GO!
AYE, MR. TOMLIN. I'LL MEET YOU AT THE GUNS WITH A CHARGE OF POWDER IN TOW!
MOMENTS LATER, THE FRENCH BEHEMOTH OPENS FIRE AND THE DEFENDER RESPONDS IN KIND...
BOOM! BOOM! BOOM! BOOM!
BOOM! BOOM! BOOM! BOOM!

BOOM!
BOOM!
STAND CLEAR!
SWAB 'ER OUT, MEN. LET'S SEND THEM ANOTHER!
BOOM!
HERE'S ANOTHER CHARGE!
CRASH!
AAUUGH!
WE'RE HIT!
BLOODY SPLINTERS! COUGH! I FEEL LIKE I'VE WRESTLED A PORCUPINE!
WILLIE, ARE YOU OKAY?!
THAT DONE IT! OUR GUN IS WRECKED!
GUN CREW, HEAD TOPSIDE AND WE'LL LEND A HAND THERE.
BEAR UP, HELMSMAN! ONCE WE'RE AHEAD OF HER, GO HARD TO STARBOARD!
THAT'LL TAKE US RIGHT INTO HER PATH!
THAT IT WILL!
YOU BOYS! BRING THAT CHAIN SHOT OVER HERE!
AYE, CAPTAIN!

Bear Up
To "bear up" meant to change course so that the ship would travel in the same direction as the wind.

Cannon Shot
There were more types of ammunition for cannons than just the traditional iron ball. Chain shot consisted of two small cannonballs joined by a short length of chain. Bar shot was two balls connected by a bar of iron. Both were used to wreck the masts and riggings of the enemy ship. Canister shot was smaller balls packed inside a tin canister, and grapeshot was balls arranged around an iron spindle and sewn into a canvas bag. These latter two types were intended to spray out when fired, much like a shotgun shell.

ON THIS COURSE THE FRENCH WILL RAM US, SIR!
THEIR CAPTAIN WON'T WRECK HIS SHIP TO STOP A LOWLY FRIGATE LIKE US! HE'LL LOOSEN SAILS AND TAKE HER ABACK TO AVOID HITTING US...
...THEN WE'LL SEND HER A BARRAGE OF CHAIN SHOT!
THIS'LL SHRED HER RIGGINGS!
OR DISMAST HER, IF WE'RE LUCKY!
IT WORKED! THEY'VE LET LOOSE THEIR SAILS TO AVOID US, SIR!
SHE'S STOPPING DEAD! NOW...
...FIRE!
BOOM! BOOM! BOOM!
BOOM! BOOM! BOOM!
BOOM! BOOM!
WE TOOK OUT THE FOREMAST!
THAT WON'T DO. SHE CAN STILL MANEUVER WITH HER MAIN- AND MIZZENMASTS INTACT. WE DON'T DARE TRY TO PASS ALONG HER SIDE TO ESCAPE TO OPEN SEA— HER GUNS WILL TEAR US TO PIECES!
WE'VE PLAYED OUR ONLY CARDS AND COME UP SHORT.
WE MUST PREPARE TO SIGNAL... OUR SURRENDER.

SUDDENLY...
LOOK!
A SHOT'S TAKEN OFF THE MAN-O'-WAR'S BOWSPRIT!
THAT DIDN'T COME FROM US.
IT CAME FROM...
...THE BATTERY!
BUT WHY WOULD THE BATTERY FIRE ON THE FRENCH SHIP?
LT. TREMAINE AND THE OTHERS—THEY MUST'VE TAKEN THE FORT!
KEEP IT UP, MEN! EVEN A THREE-DECKER CAN'T STAND AGAINST A BATTERY !
WE MANAGED TO RUN OFF WHAT WAS LEFT OF THE FRENCH TROOPS AND GET TO THESE CANNONS JUST IN TIME!
WE'RE LUCKY THE EXPLOSION THREW THEIR COMMAND INTO CHAOS.
RELOAD! LET'S SEND THEM ANOTHER ROUND OF IRON!
WE'VE BEEN GIVEN A SECOND CHANCE. LET'S NOT SQUANDER IT! LOAD UP THOSE GUNS!
AYE, AYE!

Land Cannons vs. Shipboard Cannons

A fighting ship, no matter how many guns she had on board, stood little chance against a land battery in battle. The instability of the rolling seas made precise aim difficult on a ship, and the wooden hulls of a sea vessel were much more vulnerable to damage than the stone walls of a fort. Combined with the land battery's greater elevation, this made for an uneven fight.

THEN THE MIGHTY FRENCH GIANT IS BATTERED FROM TWO SIDES BY HER INTENDED PREY AND THE CAPTURED BATTERY GUNS!

THERE GOES HER MAINMAST! SHE'LL HAVE NO CONTROL NOW!

WE'VE GOT HER. SHE'S A FISH IN A BARREL!
BOOM!
BOOM!
SHE'S HITTING THE ROCKS! SHE'S GROUNDED!
KA-CRUNCH
HER WHITE FLAG'S GONE UP! CEASE FIRE! IT'S OVER!
MY LADS, WE'VE TAKEN THE DAY!
HURRAH!
HURRAH!
HURRAH!

Spiking Cannons

Cannons had small holes, called touchholes, at the back end that led down into the barrel where the charge and shot were stuffed. The cannons were fired by touching a spark or flame to the small charge of gunpowder that led the flame down the touchhole. A cannon could be rendered useless by driving a metal spike down this touchhole until it was flush with the top of the hole, making the gun unfireable. This practice was referred to as "spiking."

HOURS LATER, WITH DUMONT NOW STRIPPED OF ITS DEFENSES AND THE MEN FROM THE SHORE PARTY SAFELY BACK ON BOARD THE SHIP, THE CREW SETS LONGBOATS AFLAME AND SENDS THEM OFF TOWARD THE COASTLINE.

GOOD WORK, LT. TREMAINE. THOSE SHIPS WILL NEVER TOUCH ENGLAND'S SHORES NOW.
NOR WILL DUMONT'S BATTERY CANNONS FIRE ON US AGAIN—WE SPIKED THE GUNS BEFORE WE ABANDONED THE FORT.
LIEUTENANT, WHAT ABOUT ALL THE PEOPLE IN THAT VILLAGE?

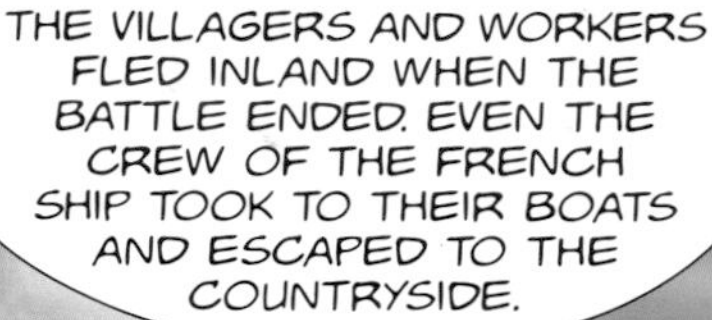
THE VILLAGERS AND WORKERS FLED INLAND WHEN THE BATTLE ENDED. EVEN THE CREW OF THE FRENCH SHIP TOOK TO THEIR BOATS AND ESCAPED TO THE COUNTRYSIDE.

YOU KNOW, SIR, EVEN THOUGH HEWITT BETRAYED US, I STILL FEEL BAD FOR HIM. AFTER ALL, HE JUST WANTED TO RETURN HOME TO HIS FAMILY.
TRUE ENOUGH, JACK...

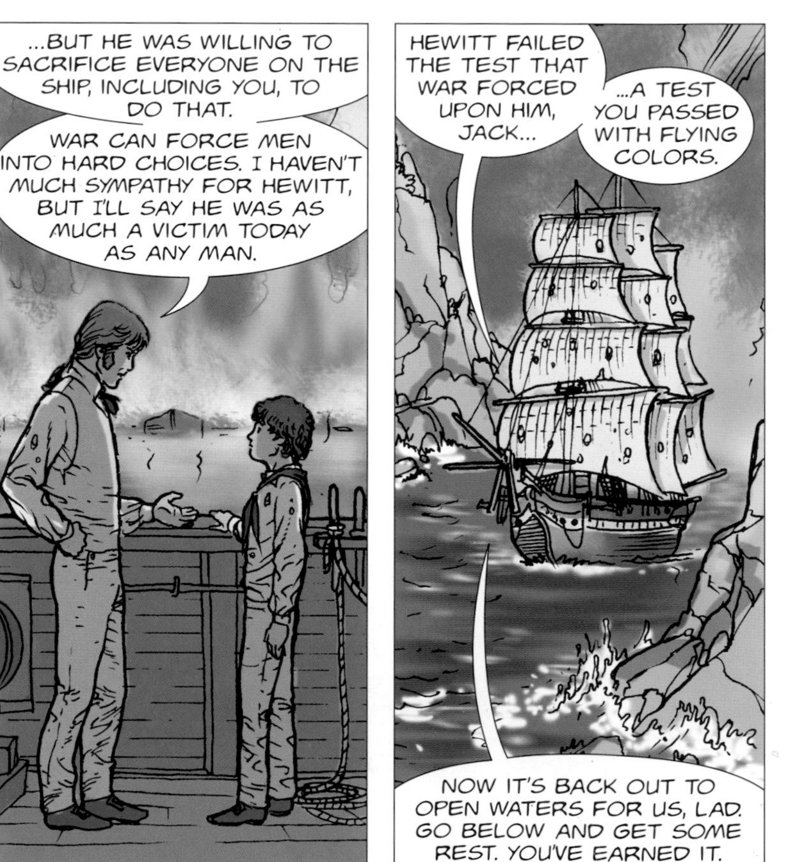
...BUT HE WAS WILLING TO SACRIFICE EVERYONE ON THE SHIP, INCLUDING YOU, TO DO THAT.
WAR CAN FORCE MEN INTO HARD CHOICES. I HAVEN'T MUCH SYMPATHY FOR HEWITT, BUT I'LL SAY HE WAS AS MUCH A VICTIM TODAY AS ANY MAN.
HEWITT FAILED THE TEST THAT WAR FORCED UPON HIM, JACK...
...A TEST YOU PASSED WITH FLYING COLORS.
NOW IT'S BACK OUT TO OPEN WATERS FOR US, LAD. GO BELOW AND GET SOME REST. YOU'VE EARNED IT.

THE SHIP'S A DISASTER!
NOT TO WORRY. SHE'S SOUND ENOUGH TO GET US BACK TO THE ADMIRAL'S FLEET.
CLEAR THIS DEBRIS OFF THE DECK.
IS THE HULL STILL WATER-TIGHT?
AYE. ALL THE HITS WERE ABOVE THE WATER-LINE.
BLIMEY, THIS RIGGING'S A TERRIBLE MESS.
THE SAILMAKERS 'LL HAVE THEIR HANDS FULL MENDING THESE HOLES.
AYE, AND THE CARPENTERS, TOO. THE PORT SIDE OF THE SHIP IS A WRECK.
WE'LL SAVE WHAT'S LEFT OF THIS SAIL. WE'RE GOING TO NEED CANVAS BAGS FOR THE DEAD.
WHAT'S THE BUTCHER'S BILL FROM TODAY?
TWELVE DEAD SO FAR...
...BUT THERE'S PLENTY MORE WOUNDED.
WILLIE! YOU'RE A WORSE MESS THAN THE SHIP!
I SWEAR THE SHIP'S SURGEON TOOK ENOUGH SPLINTERS FROM ME TO BUILD A WHOLE FRIGATE!
OUR FIRST NAVAL BATTLE AND WE LIVED TO TELL THE TALE!
I...I GUESS SO.
IT AIN'T LIKE THEY SAY, WILLIE. ALL THOSE STORIES ABOUT GLORY AND HONOR. IT AIN'T LIKE THAT.
TURNS OUT, WHEN YOU'RE IN BATTLE, ALL YOU'RE REALLY THINKING ABOUT IS STAYIN' ALIVE...
...AND TRYING NOT TO LET YOUR FRIENDS DOWN.
MAYBE THAT'S ALL "DUTY" REALLY IS.

Carpenters and Sailmakers
Sea vessels required constant repair and maintenance, so all vessels had carpenters and sailmakers on board—along with supplies of extra sail canvas and lumber.

Promotion

Many officers in the British navy were sons of the upper class. Well-connected boys might start in the coveted position of captain's servant and then work their way up to midshipman after a few years at sea. But even a young recruit not born to privilege, who started at the lowly rating of "boy, third-class," could reach midshipman status if he showed promise. From there, if he worked and studied hard, he could someday advance to the next level of a fully commissioned officer by passing the navy's lieutenant's examination. Some never managed to pass the test, and they remained midshipmen for their entire naval career. Others rose through the ranks all the way to admiral.

THE NEXT MORNING, JACK IS ASKED TO RELATE HIS STORY TO A GATHERING OF THE DEFENDER'S OFFICERS.
...AFTER ALL THAT, I HEADED BACK TO THE SHIP TO WARN YOU. THE REST YOU KNOW, SIR.
QUITE A TALE!
MR. HOYTON, AT THE LEAST IT SEEMS EVERY MAN ON THIS SHIP HAS YOU TO THANK FOR HIS CONTINUED FREEDOM.
IN FACT, I'D SAY ALL OF ENGLAND IS IN YOUR DEBT.
YOU CAME TO US FAIRLY ROUGH AT THE EDGES, LAD, BUT YOU'VE ACQUITTED YOURSELF WELL.
I EXPECT IF YOU MAINTAIN YOUR PRESENT COURSE YOU'LL MAKE A FINE MIDSHIPMAN SOMEDAY. PERHAPS EVEN AN OFFICER.
NOW I MUST WRITE A REPORT TO THE ADMIRAL FOR WHEN WE MEET UP WITH THE FLEET.
YOU'RE DISMISSED. REPORT TOPSIDE TO MR. CATES AND HELP WITH THE CLEANUP.
AYE, SIR!
I HOPE CATES ISN'T ON HIS USUAL HIGH HORSE TODAY.
YOU MEN SECURE THAT STAY. AND DRAW IN THE SLACK IN THAT LINE.
MR. HOYTON, I'VE BEEN LOOKING FOR YOU.
OH... SORRY, SIR. I'VE BEEN...
I WANT TO OFFER YOU MY RESPECTS, MISTER. HOYTON.
YOU MOST CERTAINLY EARNED THEM YESTERDAY.

NOW HOP TO! THIS SHIP WON'T SAIL HERSELF. CLIMB ALOFT AND HELP WITH HANGING THE NEW MIZZEN TOPSAIL.
AYE, SIR.
AHOY, JACK! FINISHED HAVIN' TEA AND CAKES WITH THE CAPTAIN, HAVE YOU?
WILLIE! I GUESS BEING A HUMAN PINCUSHION DOESN'T GET YOU A DAY OFF AROUND HERE, EH!
ENOUGH CLOWNIN', YOU TWO. CLIMB OUT ON THE YARD AND GIVE A HAND REEFIN' THIS SAIL.
RIGHT AWAY, MR. TOMLIN.
ALL HEAVE TOGETHER NOW.
HEAVE!
THAT'S IT, JACK. I'LL MAKE A SAILOR OUT OF YOU YET.
YOU KNOW, MR. TOMLIN, I'M STARTING TO BELIEVE YOU.

BIBLIOGRAPHY

Fremont-Barnes, Gregory. *Nelson's Sailors.* New York: Osprey Publishing, 2005.

McGregor, Tom. *The Making of Master and Commander: The Far Side of the World.* New York: W. W. Norton & Company, 2003.

O'Brian, Patrick. *Men-of-War: Life in Nelson's Navy.* New York: W. W. Norton & Company, 1974.

O'Neill, Richard, ed. *Patrick O'Brian's Navy.* London: Salamander Books, 2003.

Platt, Richard. *Stephen Biesty's Cross-Sections: Man-of-War.* New York: Dorling Kindersley, 1993.

Smith, Digby. *An Illustrated Encyclopedia of Uniforms of the Napoleonic Wars.* London: Lorenz Books, 2007.

RECOMMENDED READING

Forester, C. S. The Horatio Hornblower series of novels, starting with *Mr. Midshipman Hornblower* (New York: Back Bay Books, 1966).

O'Brian, Patrick. The Aubrey-Maturin series of novels, starting with *Master and Commander* (New York: W. W. Norton & Company, 1970).

SPECIAL THANKS TO

William N. Peterson, Senior Curator, Mystic Seaport.

G. P. PUTNAM'S SONS

A division of Penguin Young Readers Group.

Published by The Penguin Group. Penguin Group (USA) Inc., 375 Hudson Street, New York, NY 10014, U.S.A. Penguin Group (Canada), 90 Eglinton Avenue East, Suite 700, Toronto, Ontario M4P 2Y3, Canada (a division of Pearson Penguin Canada Inc.). Penguin Books Ltd, 80 Strand, London WC2R 0RL, England. Penguin Ireland, 25 St. Stephen's Green, Dublin 2, Ireland (a division of Penguin Books Ltd.). Penguin Group (Australia), 250 Camberwell Road, Camberwell, Victoria 3124, Australia (a division of Pearson Australia Group Pty Ltd). Penguin Books India Pvt Ltd, 11 Community Centre, Panchsheel Park, New Delhi - 110 017, India. Penguin Group (NZ), 67 Apollo Drive, Rosedale, North Shore 0632, New Zealand (a division of Pearson New Zealand Ltd). Penguin Books (South Africa) (Pty) Ltd, 24 Sturdee Avenue, Rosebank, Johannesburg 2196, South Africa. Penguin Books Ltd, Registered Offices: 80 Strand, London WC2R 0RL, England.

The art was created by scanning ink drawings done on bristol board into Adobe Photoshop and coloring them using a Wacom tablet.

Library of Congress Control Number: 2009932801.

ISBN 978-0-399-25089-7   10 9 8 7 6 5 4 3 2 1

HMS DEFENDER
5
6
7
8
9
10
11
12
13
14
15
16
17
18